14.95

The·Night·Book

The · Night · Book

PICTURES · BY · WILLIAM · PÈNE DU BOIS

FOR
CHRISSIE WHITNEY
SCHMIDT

Clarkson N. Potter, Inc./Publishers / NEW YORK   DISTRIBUTED BY CROWN PUBLISHERS, INC.

Once there was a little girl who was afraid of the night. When she lay in bed she thought about the day, and to get to sleep she counted bright sheep leaping in sunny meadows.

S he kept her night-light on just in case she woke up.
She didn't want to open her eyes and see nothing but dark.
And her dog, whose name was Sunshine, kept guard by the
window to chase away monsters.

One summer night while the little girl slept, the rising
moon caught a glimpse of her. "That's the little girl who's
afraid of the night," the Moon said. "I'll have to wake her up.
I don't want her to think the night is scary."

W oo woo," said the Moon, just like an owl,
and the little girl woke up.
"Hello," the Moon said, not wanting to frighten her.
But the little girl hid under the covers.

C ome on out," said the Moon. "There's lots to see." The little girl tiptoed to the window and peeked at the smiling moon. "I'll send down a moonbeam to show you the way and a moon banister for you to hold on to."

S o the little girl and her dog Sunshine went out into the night.

L ook over there," the Moon said, and sent another moonbeam
 down to shed more light. The little girl saw a bush called
a night jasmine covered with yellow flowers.

And standing very still next to it was a bird.
It was a black-crested night heron.

H ere," said the Moon. The little girl looked and saw
a night crawler, which is a worm.

And she saw a trellis of trumpet flowers closed up against the dark.

And a little cloud of moths that had come out to circle the street-lamp.

Come on," the Moon said. "Just think of me as the night sun," and his moonbeam led her to the edge of the garden. The little girl saw the night watchman making sure all the houses and all the boats on the dock were safe.

A man on a yacht was drinking a nightcap, which is a bedtime
drink for grown-ups. The man looked happy.
He waved and that made the little girl smile.
She began to think how silly it is to be afraid of the night.

"Well, isn't it nice out here," said the Moon with

Want to see something funny?" said the Moon, pointing to the house next door. A man was leaning over his desk writing.

N o, I don't," said the little girl.
"He's writing a book about a little girl who went out into the
night and was so pleased with what she saw that she was no
longer afraid," said the Moon.

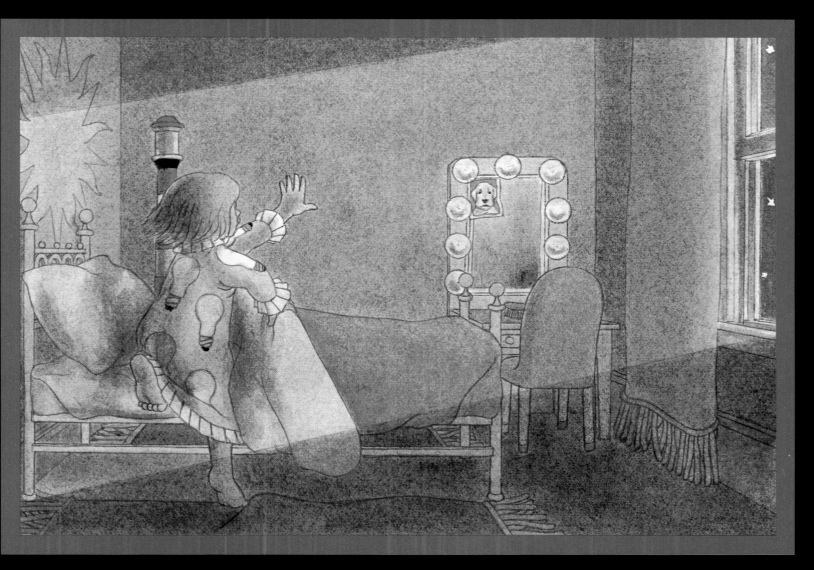

He's right," said the little girl. "I'm not afraid of the night any more." And she went back to her room, got into bed, and fell asleep. The Moon hurried away across the night sky.

Before long the sun rose and nothing that the little girl had seen in the night was still there. She looked and looked but couldn't find a thing, so she waited with Sunshine on the back porch for the Moon and the night to come back.

THE END

Published by Clarkson N. Potter, Inc., One Park Avenue, New York, New York 10016 and simultaneously in
Canada by General Publishing Company Limited. CLARKSON N. POTTER, POTTER and
colophon are trademarks of Clarkson N. Potter, Inc.

Manufactured in Belgium by Henri Proost & CIE PVBA
Designed by Carl Barile

Library of Congress Cataloging in Publication Data

Strand, Mark.
The night book.

Summary: The rising moon sees a little girl who is afraid of the night and sends down a special moonbeam
to show her the many wondrous things to see during the dark hours.
[1. Night — Fiction.   2. Fear — Fiction.   3. Moon — Fiction]
I. Du Bois, William Pène. ill.   II. Title.
PZ7.S8967Ni   1985   [E]   85-9377

ISBN 0-517-55047-4
10 9 8 7 6 5 4 3 2 1
First Edition

Pre Sch - 1
wright
fear
moon

1985